Survivor

written by
Alison Donald

Illustrated by
Michelle Simpson

Chapter 1

"Tilly! Are you coming outside? We're all in the driveway!"

My sister, Josie, was shouting at me from the front step.

Survivor

'Survivor'
An original concept by Alison Donald
© Alison Donald 2022

Illustrated by Michelle Simpson

Published by MAVERICK ARTS PUBLISHING LTD
Studio 11, City Business Centre, 6 Brighton Road,
Horsham, West Sussex, RH13 5BB
© Maverick Arts Publishing Limited May 2022
+44 (0)1403 256941

A CIP catalogue record for this book is available at the British Library.

ISBN 978-1-84886-885-4

www.maverickbooks.co.uk

This book is rated as: Grey Band (Guided Reading)

"Maybe later," I called from the living room without looking up. I was in the middle of a very intense computer game. I'd just settled in for a perfect Saturday morning. I was nestled into the sofa like a squirrel about to hibernate. I had my snuggly blue fleece blanket and my laptop.

"C'mon, we're playing Hide and Seek Zombies and we could really use another person," she said.

I looked up. Hide and Seek Zombies *did* sound like fun. But then I'd have to leave my cosy blanket and I'd also have to talk to everyone. When I didn't say much, my big sister Josie would say, "Oh, don't mind Tilly, she's just shy." And then I would get even *more* shy.

"No thanks," I called out as I re-focused on the screen. My avatar was climbing down a steep mountain in the Arctic. I needed to reach the bottom before I froze or before my food and water ran out.

It was nail-biting stuff. And it was all down to me to figure out how to fight the elements, and how to save myself.

The great thing about playing *Survivor* was that I could be someone else. I could be a hero instead of Tilly: a normal girl who got so shy that she sometimes froze like a rabbit and didn't know what to say.

"Go on, Tilly, go outside. Get off your screen," Mum called from the kitchen.

What was it with parents always wanting kids to get off of their screens?

I got back in the game. My avatar was wearing shoes with spikes on them to balance on the ice. I saw a small cave and crawled inside it to get some rest before I descended the mountain.

"It's good for you to play outside. And next week, you'll be outdoors all week," Mum insisted.

"Outdoors all week? What do you mean?" I called out.

I sorted through the supplies while I was in the cave to see if I could lighten my load. I pulled out some empty food containers and left them in the cave. Every bit mattered. If the bag was too heavy, I might not have the strength to make it to the bottom.

"Next week, you're going camping!"

I put the laptop down and went into the kitchen.

"What!?" I demanded.

"I've signed you up for Explorers camp," Mum said. "And there's no devices allowed."

This was just the *absolute* worst.

Chapter 2

"Mum, I *really* don't want to go to this camp on Friday," I said for the umpteenth time as I climbed out of the car on Tuesday evening. Mum was dropping me off at the village hall for the weekly Explorers meeting, the local girls' youth group.

"Sometimes you have to trust me, Tilly. I really think you'll love it once you're there."

I rolled my eyes and slammed the car door. No matter what I said, Mum wasn't changing her mind. It really did look like I'd be camping on Friday.

The hall floor was shiny, the lights were too bright and the room smelled like sweat from the previous dance class.

Everyone was painting. I spotted an empty seat beside Jasmin. She was the other 'quiet' girl but I didn't know her very well.

Hana, our leader, promised us a fun art activity this week. I loved painting and I got lost in the pink and purple colours of my blossom tree. I almost didn't hear Jasmin speak.

"Are you going on the camping trip this Friday?" she asked.

"Yeah, unfortunately," I said. "My mum is insisting but..." I lowered my voice and leant over my painting, "I really don't want to go. I don't actually like camping," I sighed.

"Me neither," said Jasmin. "Last time we learned how to paddle canoes but it was cold and raining."

This was the longest conversation I'd ever had with Jasmin. Maybe we had things in common—other than being shy.

"Let's ask if we can share a bunk," I suggested.

Jasmin grinned, and I smiled back. I wasn't one hundred percent sure, but it *felt* like I'd found a friend.

A cackle of laughter erupted from Seema and Morgan, cutting through the warm, fuzzy feeling I was having.

"Who doesn't like camping?" asked Seema in a loud voice.

"And, if you don't like camping, why would you be in Explorers in the first place?" Morgan joined in. They both glared at us and sniggered again.

I looked at Jasmin and shook my head. Seema and Morgan were in the 'cool girl' group at Explorers. They always managed to give dirty looks or hiss rude comments when Hana wasn't looking.

The reasons not to go camping were stacking up faster than the pile of dirty clothes in my room: 1) No gaming, 2) no gaming and 3) spending time with the mean, cool girls. I was dreading Friday more and more.

Chapter 3

The campground was set in a forest near a lake. I breathed in the smell of pine needles and wood while I unpacked in our cabin. Jasmin and I flipped a coin to decide who would get the top bunk and she won. I didn't mind though, I was just happy Jasmin and I were bunk mates.

Once we were unpacked, Hana whisked us off to the activity centre. Our first activity was treetop walking.

As the instructor clipped on our harnesses, Jasmin turned to me. Her eyes were wide. "No one mentioned anything about heights!"

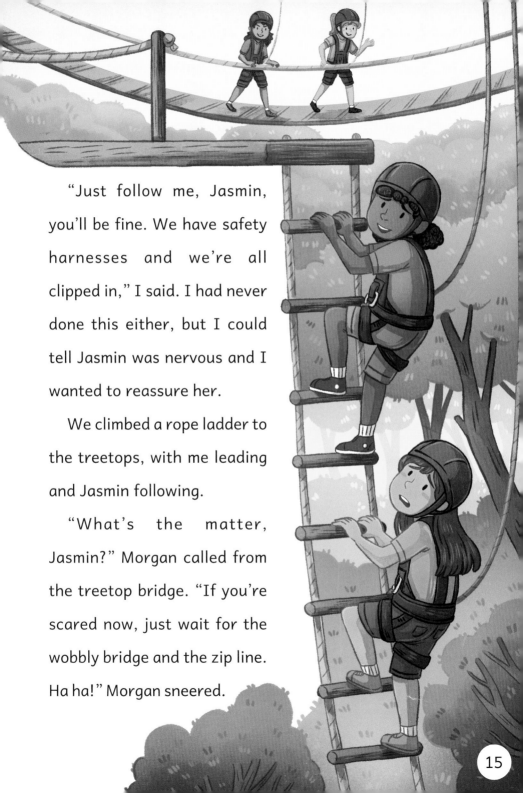

"Just follow me, Jasmin, you'll be fine. We have safety harnesses and we're all clipped in," I said. I had never done this either, but I could tell Jasmin was nervous and I wanted to reassure her.

We climbed a rope ladder to the treetops, with me leading and Jasmin following.

"What's the matter, Jasmin?" Morgan called from the treetop bridge. "If you're scared now, just wait for the wobbly bridge and the zip line. Ha ha!" Morgan sneered.

"Ignore her, Jasmin," I said. "You can do this." Jasmin took tiny baby steps across the first rope bridge.

"I did it!" she squealed.

"See! It's actually fun, and it's nice and cool up here in the treetops."

We paused for a moment and heard birds tweeting back and forth, like they were having a conversation. A red squirrel ran past us with an acorn in its mouth and we both laughed.

"Thanks, Tilly. I wouldn't have made it across the bridge without you," Jasmin said.

After lunch, we headed over to an empty field filled with go-karts. Our instructor gave us a lesson on how to drive them around the track.

When it was time to drive, I couldn't remember which pedal made the kart go and which pedal made the kart stop. The go-kart stalled and bolted backwards. Morgan and Seema burst into laughter when they spotted my mistake. I lowered my head and wished I could slide down and disappear.

Jasmin was doing laps around the track when she saw me struggling. She came over to help.

"Just ignore them," she said. "This one's the accelerator, that one's the brake," she explained. "Take it slow and you'll be fine."

I tried again. The go-kart spluttered and bolted forward.

"Don't push so hard on the pedal!" Jasmin called out.

I eased up on the pedal and soon I was moving forward onto the track with everyone else. Jasmin and I drove around the track together. I couldn't believe it! I was doing it! As long as I ignored Morgan and Seema, this was shaping up to be a great day! Maybe camping was my thing after all.

We had a campfire with marshmallows that night before heading back to the cabin for bed. In the morning, we would be packing up and heading into the deep woods for a canoe trip where we would camp in tents. While we brushed our teeth, the cool girls bragged.

"Camping in a tent in the forest is so amazing! I've camped so many times with my family," boasted Morgan.

"We're basically experts. This Explorers camping trip is too easy for us," Seema chimed in.

Jasmin and I brushed in silence. Neither of us wanted to go into the woods to camp—especially with Morgan and Seema. I had a funny feeling in the pit of my stomach that something was about to go terribly wrong.

Chapter 4

At breakfast the next morning, I pushed my eggs around the plate with my fork. We had already packed: our clothing, two tents, and all our supplies so that everything could be carried by the group on our backs. It was already warm in the food hall which meant that it would be scorching later on. The thought of being stuck in a canoe in this heat didn't sound fun at all. I suddenly missed my cosy Saturday mornings, where I could game at home on the sofa with my fuzzy, blue blanket.

After breakfast, we put on our backpacks and carried the canoes overhead to the lake. The canoe was heavy and the mosquitoes were biting.

I let go of the canoe with one hand to scratch my arm and the canoe dipped.

"Don't drop the canoe!" Morgan scolded.

I rolled my eyes.

Finally, we put the canoes down and rested for a few minutes. Hana went over the plan.

"We'll be paddling for about an hour to get to the campsite. We'll go in groups of four, and I'll be in the front canoe to guide the way. If anyone gets separated, the safest thing to do is paddle to shore as soon as you can and call me on the walkie-talkie. Understood?"

We all nodded.

I hoped I would be in Hana's group. Then I wouldn't have to worry about this kind of thing. I also hoped I'd be with Jasmin.

"Canoe Number One will be: Tilly, Jasmin..."

Jasmin and I high-fived. I was so happy we would be together. Now if the other people could be anyone other than Morgan or Seema that would be perfect.

"...Morgan and Seema."

What? No! I thought as Hana divided the rest of the girls into their canoes.

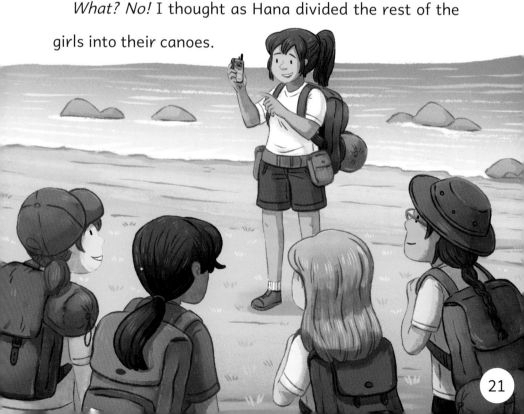

"I will be in Canoe Number Four with anyone whose name I haven't said," Hana pointed to one of the other canoes.

Great, I thought. Not only was I not with Hana but I was stuck with Morgan and Seema. I took my paddle and sighed.

Hana handed Jasmin a walkie-talkie.

"At least it's only an hour," Jasmin said as we lowered and pushed the canoe out, "and then we don't have to spend any more time with Morgan and Seema."

I wanted to believe her, but I also knew that a lot could go wrong in an hour.

Chapter 5

We all set off together. Jasmin and I were paddling in the front of our canoe with Morgan and Seema in the back. Hana's canoe was paddling beside us with the rest of the group's canoes close behind. Soon, Hana's canoe overtook us and led the way. One by one, the other Explorers' canoes passed us. We were struggling to stay on course. We were struggling to even move the canoe forward!

"Paddle harder!" Morgan yelled as the canoe spun in circles.

"Seema needs to steer!" I called in frustration. We could paddle as fast as we liked but unless Seema steered us in the right direction, we were stuck.

"Girls," Hana called out.

"Work together."

I rolled my eyes. That was the problem. Morgan and Seema were not team players.

Finally, the canoe moved forwards and we were catching up with Hana and the rest of the group. The river narrowed. We paddled along in awkward silence. A fork in the river was coming up, as it widened and then separated around a group of trees. Hana veered left, but I could see that our canoe was going right.

"Steer the canoe left. We're going the wrong way," I insisted.

"I know what I'm doing!" Seema snapped.

Why couldn't Seema just listen? I wished I was steering.

"Guys!" I yelled. "Quickly! We're going the wrong way!"

"Don't tell her what to do!" Morgan shouted.

"Girls!" Hana shouted from her canoe. "Work as a team! Seema, pull your paddle in."

"We're moving to the right!" Jasmin cried. "Do something!"

"I'm trying!" Seema shouted.

Soon Seema and Morgan were bickering.

"Pull your paddle in more!" Morgan said.

"I'm doing it as much as I can!" Seema huffed.

"Then, *you're* doing it wrong!" Morgan argued.

"Shut up!" Seema snapped.

The current in the river was moving faster. We were running out of time.

"Enough!" I shouted. "Dig in your paddle and stop the canoe, Seema!"

But my words weren't quick enough. Our canoe sailed past the fork in the river and drifted down the right-hand route. Hana's canoe was completely out of sight now.

"Great!" Jasmin said.

We tried to go backwards but the canoe continued to move forwards. Soon, there was a patch of shore big enough for us to stop.

"Jasmin, move your paddle in the other direction so we can get closer," I asked.

"I can't wait to get out of this canoe!" Morgan declared and she lunged forward in the canoe in an attempt to jump onto shore, causing the canoe to tip. We didn't have time to steady ourselves and we all fell overboard.

"Morgan, what have you done?!" I cried. "Never make sudden movements in a canoe!"

We all got to our feet quickly in the shallow water. The water was cool and refreshing but also a shock! Why did Morgan do that? We pulled the canoe onto the shore, absolutely soaked.

"Let's set up camp here until the others find us," I said.

"Great idea," Jasmin agreed. "I'll radio Hana to let her know we're okay... Except... Oh no!" she cried as she reached into her vest pocket and pulled out a dripping wet walkie-talkie.

She pressed a few buttons but it was clearly dead.

Morgan and Seema gasped.

"This is all your fault, Morgan, for tipping the canoe!" Jasmin cried.

This was not good. I needed everyone to stay calm.

"Don't worry, Hana and the rest of the group will find us," I said calmly, but inside I was worried. Our canoe had drifted quite far away and I wasn't exactly sure how Hana would find us without us guiding her through the walkie-talkie.

The girls looked at me in disbelief.

I glanced around at the rugged landscape. My stomach started to growl. It had been a long time since breakfast.

"Let's have something to eat," I suggested.

"Hana has all the food and cooking supplies," Morgan groaned.

"What are we going to do?" Seema wailed.

We all stared at each other as the realisation sank in that we were completely on our own in the middle of the forest with no food. Morgan started to cry. I felt like crying too. What were we going to do?

Chapter 6

I stood beside the river and thought about what to do. If I was playing *Survivor*, I would try to do small things to improve the situation until eventually I could solve the bigger problems. I couldn't tell Hana how to find us, but maybe I could help us with other things.

"There's not much we can do about telling Hana where we are right now, but we can look after ourselves," I said. "Let's start with setting up camp. Hana said we should stay put. Morgan and Seema, can you show us how to put up the tent?"

Morgan wiped her tears. "Yes, I can do that. I always help my family set up the tent when we go camping."

"That's great. Let's get started," I said.

We spread out the ground sheet and Morgan showed us how to use the pegs and mallet to secure the sheets to the ground. Morgan got out the poles and explained that they were colour-coded. She was knowledgeable and good at explaining things. The four of us actually worked well together—once we listened to each other! When the tent was up, we unzipped the doors and windows. Next, we unrolled our beds.

"This is great!" I said. "We have shelter and a place to sleep."

Seema's eyes grew wide. "I don't want to sleep here tonight on our own."

I thought back to *Survivor*. It was always important to make sure everyone felt calm.

"Don't worry, Seema, I'm sure Hana will be here before dark. She must know these woods really well," I said. I wasn't sure what would happen, but we had to be hopeful.

Seema nodded.

"Let's gather wood so we can set up a fire for tonight. A fire will keep things bright as the sun goes down," I suggested.

We wandered around the woods and gathered sticks, twigs and small branches.

"Let's set the fire up over here," Seema suggested, gesturing near the tent and several trees.

"It would be much safer to set up the fire pit away from the trees and away from the tent. The sandy beach would be perfect," I suggested.

Seema nodded. "Yes, of course. Good idea, Tilly," she said.

Good idea? Was I hearing things? Was Seema actually agreeing with me?

Jasmin and I found a safe spot in the sand far away from any trees and far away from the tent. Next, we stood the thicker branches and sticks on their ends and put the small twigs in between as kindling. Lastly, we gathered stones and built a circle with them around the wood and kindling. We had the makings of a safe fire pit. Another small job done.

But it was getting hard to ignore the aching in my stomach. I was sure others felt the same.

"Does anyone have any water or snacks in their bags?" I asked.

Seema and Morgan shook their heads.

"Oh! I think I have a bottle of water in my bag. And marshmallows!" Jasmin offered.

"Perfect," I said, though what I really wanted was a burger. "Everyone have a drink. I'll light the fire." I had found matches in a waterproof bag that was packed in with the tent.

"We'll roast marshmallows," I suggested. It was already starting to get dark and I worried that everyone might get scared when the sun went down.

We told funny ghost stories to pass the time but there was still a gnawing in my stomach despite the marshmallows. Why hadn't Hana turned up yet? Were we really about to spend the night out here alone?

The temperature dropped and the marshmallows were long gone. We put the fire out before it got too dark and headed back to the tent.

"Okay everyone, I have a surprise for you," Morgan said just before we stepped into the tent. Oh no, what was she up to? But suddenly, the tent was lit up with fairy lights.

"It's beautiful!" I cried.

"We have light!" Jasmin said.

"When my family goes camping, we bring waterproof, battery-operated lights to light up the inside and outside of the tent. I brought them as a surprise!" Morgan said.

Morgan's whole face was lit up too. Her love of camping was obvious and it was a pleasant surprise to see her being thoughtful.

We settled into our beds and an awkward silence fell over us in the sparkly light of the tent.

"I'm scared," Seema whispered.

"Me too," Morgan replied.

"Me three," Jasmin said.

I was scared too. But I wasn't going to show it.

"We've done a brilliant job tonight setting up camp and having a campfire. We've got this!" I said firmly. "It's just one night."

Everyone nodded in agreement. We had accomplished a lot but sleeping alone in the woods at night was something completely different.

"Does anyone want to hear about this game called *Survivor* that I like to play?" I asked. Maybe a distraction would help everyone to feel less afraid.

Everyone nodded again.

I talked about how I'd dodged venomous snakes in rainforests, and battled the ice and frost in Antarctica. I told them about running from elephants in the African jungles and keeping away from shark-infested waters in the Caribbean.

When I finally ran out of tales of survival, we lay in silence and listened to the patter of woodland creatures and the hooting of owls. I pulled the covers up under my chin and wished for our survival.

Chapter 7

Suddenly, we saw bright lights. I heard tyres crunching in the dirt and the hum of an engine.

"Help has arrived!" I said, hoping it was true.

"Girls?" a familiar voice called when the engine turned off. "It's me, Hana."

We jumped up and unzipped the tent as fast as we could. We rushed over and hugged her all at once.

"I am so glad you're alright. As soon as we got to the woodland camp, I tried radioing you but there was no answer. I'm so sorry we took so long to find you. I had to contact the main camp before leaving otherwise the other girls would have been alone. What happened to the walkie-talkie I gave you?"

In the glow of the fairy lights, we all looked at Morgan. She hung her head.

Jasmin and I exchanged a knowing look. We didn't want to tell on Morgan, but we also didn't want to be blamed for what happened.

"It's my fault," Morgan said. "I stood up in the canoe and tipped it, and then the walkie-talkie didn't work. I'm sorry."

My jaw dropped. Had Morgan just taken responsibility

and told the truth?

"Thank you for telling the truth, Morgan. Luckily, you're all safe. You girls have done an amazing job setting up camp!" Hana said. "Well done."

"Tilly gets the credit for that," Seema said. "She was calm and she encouraged us to stay positive and keep going."

Wow! Was this the same Seema who was laughing at me yesterday because I couldn't drive the go-kart?

"Thanks," I said. "But Seema and Morgan were the ones who showed us how to put up the tent," I pointed out.

"Excellent job, everyone. You all must be hungry. We have burgers and hot dogs at the campsite and an extra tent all set up for you. Pack your things up and hop in."

We quickly took the tent down and piled everything in the truck. When we arrived at the real campsite, the rest of the group cheered.

"Were you scared?" Sally asked.

"How did you know how to put the tent up?" Nat asked.

"Were there any bears?" Bree wondered.

Hana laughed. "I'm sure the girls will answer all your questions, but first let's cook them some hot dogs and burgers. They must be starving."

Food and water had never tasted so good. We answered some of the questions and then we all climbed into the tents for bedtime.

I suddenly felt exhausted and a dreamless sleep washed over me.

Chapter 8

The next morning, we had stacks of pancakes and bacon for breakfast before we packed. I felt so relieved that we were okay. But I also felt unsettled. As Jasmin and I walked back to the tent I wondered: would Morgan and Seema continue to be nice or would they go back to being horrible to Jasmin and me, like before?

Morgan and Seema approached us and interrupted my thoughts, as if they could read my mind.

"We just wanted to apologise," Morgan said.

"For being horrible," Seema added.

I looked at Jasmin and she looked just as surprised as me.

"When you said you didn't like camping, we thought we could never be friends, but it turns out that you're both really nice..."

"You really helped us to stay calm with all of your *Survivor* stories," Seema added.

I looked at my feet. Knowing what to say wasn't always easy for me. Before this camping trip, I wouldn't have told Morgan how I felt. But I had taken charge in a scary situation and kept everyone safe. It gave me the confidence to reply.

"Apology accepted. I think we'll all get along fine, as long as no one stands up in the canoe..." I joked.

Everyone laughed.

"Don't worry," Morgan said. "It will never happen again."

"It *would* be fun to hang out together sometime though, you know, outside of Explorers," Seema offered.

Everyone paused. We didn't go to the same school so it would be tricky to find a way. Suddenly, I had an idea.

"I have the perfect plan for getting together," I said, "and I think you're going to love it!"

A few weeks later, I was back at home and it was like I'd never left. I nestled into the sofa with my blue, fuzzy blanket and my laptop. I clicked on *Survivor* but this time, Jasmin, Morgan and Seema were already logged on and waiting for me. We gamed together now every week. It was much more fun gaming with friends.

"Tilly! Our neighbours are outside and we're playing Hide and Seek Zombies!" Josie shouted.

"I'll be there in ten minutes!" I called out, and I set a timer so I wouldn't forget.

We chose a jungle setting this time in *Survivor* and we were trying to survive amongst venomous snakes and deadly mosquitoes. I learned that I liked camping but I preferred the life and death stuff when it was just a game.

When the timer dinged, I signed off and went outside. My sister and the kids from my street were talking in the driveway.

"We're bored of playing Hide and Seek Zombies," Josie said.

"What should we do?" the boy from next-door asked.

"I've got an idea," I said. "Follow me."

I opened the side gate and we entered the back garden.

"Who wants to toast marshmallows?" I asked.

"Me!" everyone cried at once.

I asked Mum to light the fire pit and she agreed—even though it was the middle of the afternoon.

While we roasted marshmallows, everyone took turns telling a ghost story.

"Tilly, it's your turn," Josie said.

I didn't feel shy. I didn't go quiet like I usually did. I knew exactly what I wanted to say.

"One dark night," I started, "a group of girls found themselves all alone in the deep, dark woods…"

You could hear a pin drop. All eyes were on me and everyone was waiting to hear more.

"And this is the story of how they survived…"

Discussion Points

1. Who invites Tilly outside in the beginning?

2. What do Tilly and Jasmin see in the treetops?

a) A red squirrel

b) A brown owl

c) A woodpecker

3. What was your favourite part of the story?

4. How do Tilly, Jasmin, Morgan and Seema get separated from the rest of the group?

5. Why do you think Tilly's knowledge of *Survivor* helped her in real life?

6. Who was your favourite character and why?

7. There were moments in the story when Tilly had to **be a leader**. Where do you think the story shows this most?

8. What do you think happens after the end of the story?

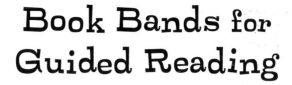

Book Bands for Guided Reading

Pink

Red

Yellow

Blue

Green

Orange

Turquoise

Purple

Gold

White

Lime

Brown

Grey

The Institute of Education book banding system is a scale of colours that reflects the various levels of reading difficulty. The bands are assigned by taking into account the content, the language style, the layout and phonics. Word, phrase and sentence level work is also taken into consideration.

The Maverick Readers Scheme is a bright, attractive range of books covering the pink to grey bands. All of these books have been book banded for guided reading to the industry standard and edited by a leading educational consultant.

To view the whole Maverick Readers scheme, visit our website at

www.maverickearlyreaders.com

Or scan the QR code to view our scheme instantly!

Maverick Chapter Readers
(From Lime to Grey Band)